W9-CCP-181

Ex-Library: Friends of
Lake County Public Library

To Adèle

J.M.

To Amelia

N.B.

With thanks to
Daphne Elverson
for the use of her
collection of
dollhouses

3 3113 01358 5734

Text copyright © 1993 by Jan Mark
Illustrations copyright © 1993 by Nicola Bayley

All rights reserved.

First U.S. edition 1993
Published in Great Britain in 1993 by
Walker Books Ltd., London.

Library of Congress Cataloging-in-Publication Data

Mark, Jan.
Fun with Mrs. Thumb / Jan Mark ; illustrated by Nicola Bayley.—
1st U.S. ed.
Summary: A cat taunts the inhabitant of a dollhouse until
a human comes to offer him his dinner.
ISBN 1-56402-247-1
[1. Cats—Fiction.   2. Stories in rhyme.]
I. Bayley, Nicola, ill.   II. Title.
PZ8.3.M39146Fu   1993
[E]—dc20   92-54955

10 9 8 7 6 5 4 3 2 1

Printed in Hong Kong.

The pictures in this book were done in watercolor.

Candlewick Press
2067 Massachusetts Avenue
Cambridge, Massachusetts 02140

Fun With
Mrs. Thumb

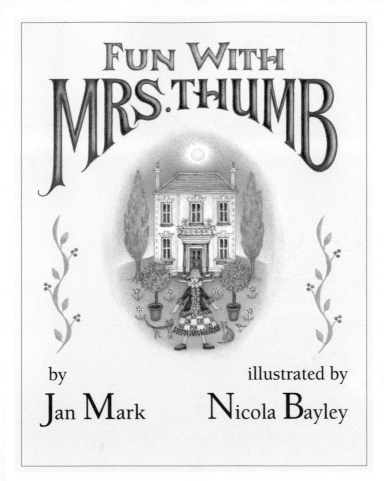

by

illustrated by

Jan Mark

Nicola Bayley

CANDLEWICK PRESS
CAMBRIDGE, MASSACHUSETTS

LAKE COUNTY PUBLIC LIBRARY

H ere is the house

and here am I . . .

And here is
Mrs. Thumb.

Mrs. Thumb
sits and sews.
Nobody knows
that I have come
to play with Mrs. Thumb.

Mrs. Thumb,

Mrs. Thumb!

Leave your chair

and cross the room.

Let me into

your house.

I will not eat you

—promise!

I am full of milk

and mouse.

Dear Mrs. Thumb,
come out to play.
See what I have
brought today:
my lovely fur,
my lovely purr,
my lovely paws,
full of claws.

Here I come.

Oh, lovely me,

oh, *lucky* Mrs. Thumb.

Do you like

hide-and-seek?

Let's play you're

a mouse —

I'll bite, you squeak.

Off you go!

Bumpety-

bumpety-bump.

I love this game.

Aren't you glad I came?

Real mice

squeak and skip

when I nip,

so . . .

when I pounce,

you bounce.

I'll toss you in the air,

there —

why don't you try

to be a bird and fly?

Now someone's come
to rescue you.
Unfair! Unfair!
They keep doing that
with my mice, too.

Cheer up.

Here's one last swipe

before they shut you in.

I have to go now—

someone is opening a tin.

Ah, meat is good,
and milk is nice.
That Mrs. Thumb is
only made of wood—
unlike mice.

But in a while

I'll go and say

good night to

Mrs. Thumb.

I'll look through

the window

of her room

with my smile

and all my lovely teeth.